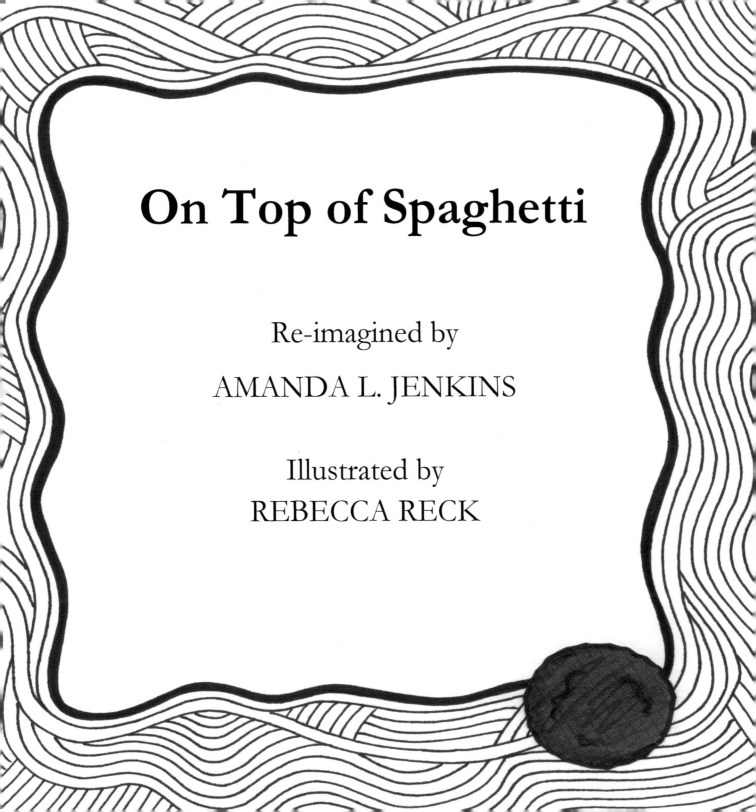

On Top of Spaghetti

Re-imagined by

AMANDA L. JENKINS

Illustrated by

REBECCA RECK

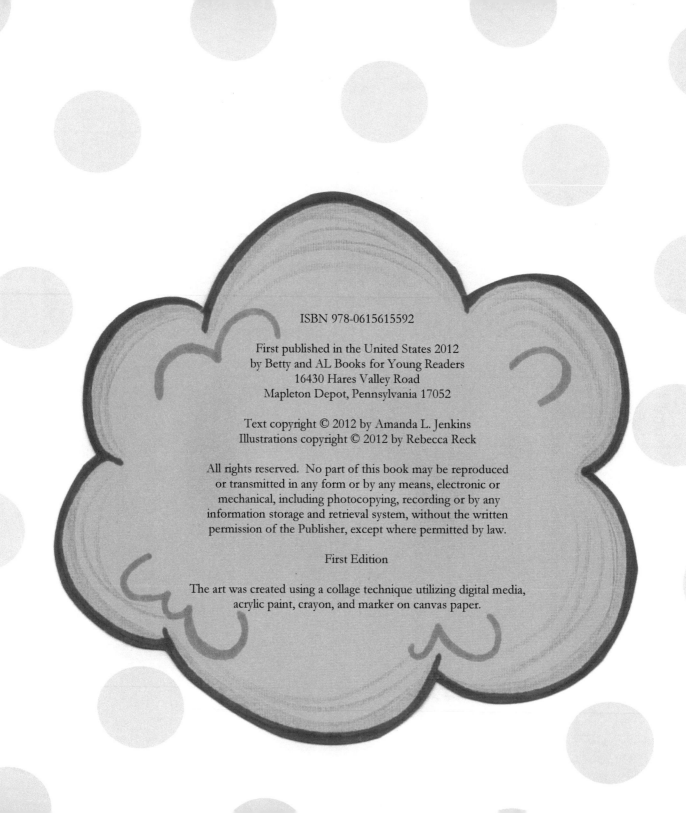

ISBN 978-0615615592

First published in the United States 2012
by Betty and AL Books for Young Readers
16430 Hares Valley Road
Mapleton Depot, Pennsylvania 17052

First Edition

The art was created using a collage technique utilizing digital media,
acrylic paint, crayon, and marker on canvas paper.

To Great Dads

On top of spaghetti
all covered with cheese…

It rolled off the table and onto the floor.

It kept right on going…

right out the front door.

It traveled the sidewalk.

It passed by a bush.

It fell into a cool stream,
where it turned into mush.

As a fish came and ate it,
it made me holler and cry.

I went back to my warm house
and let out a sigh.

I missed that poor meatball.

I missed it with my whole heart.

Yet I quickly forgot it,

To the tune of "On Top of Old Smoky"

Traditional American

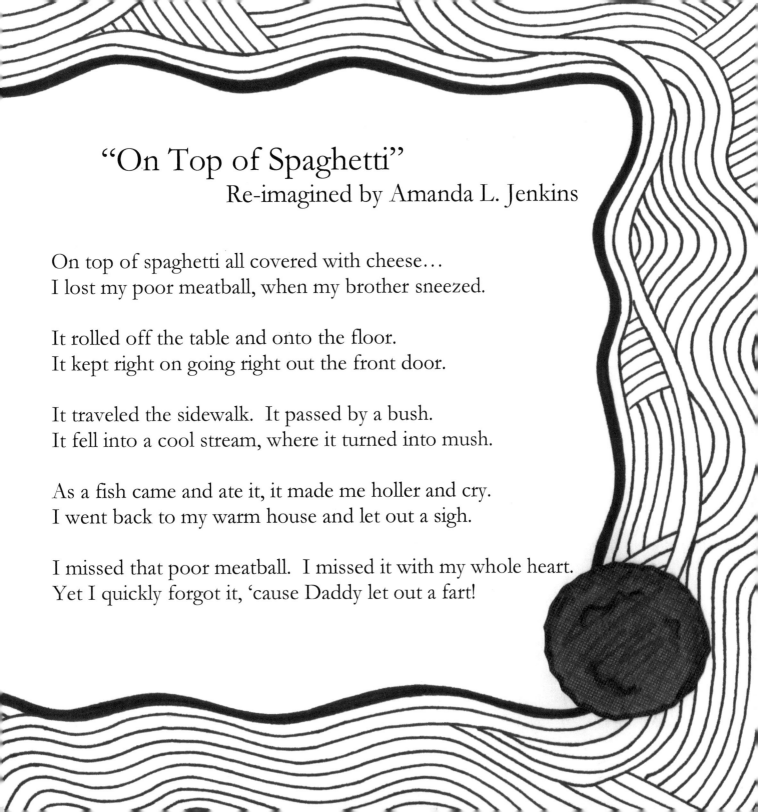

"On Top of Spaghetti"
Re-imagined by Amanda L. Jenkins

On top of spaghetti all covered with cheese…
I lost my poor meatball, when my brother sneezed.

It rolled off the table and onto the floor.
It kept right on going right out the front door.

It traveled the sidewalk. It passed by a bush.
It fell into a cool stream, where it turned into mush.

As a fish came and ate it, it made me holler and cry.
I went back to my warm house and let out a sigh.

I missed that poor meatball. I missed it with my whole heart.
Yet I quickly forgot it, 'cause Daddy let out a fart!